Here's HANK

The New York... series by
Henry Winkler & Lin Oliver

The Soggy, Foggy Campout

ILLUSTRATED BY SCOTT GARRETT

Penguin Workshop

For Ricardo and Leticia—thank you for everything—HW

For Leslie Tomasini, remembering
all those great campouts—LO

For Bobbie and Jack Carty . . .
you're in a book!—SG

W

PENGUIN WORKSHOP
An Imprint of Penguin Random House LLC, New York

The publisher does not have any control over and does not assume
any responsibility for author or third-party websites or their content.

Typeset in Dyslexie Font B.V.
Dyslexie Font B.V. was designed by Christian Boer.

Library of Congress Control Number: 2016011690

ISBN 9780448486604 (pbk)   10 9 8 7 6 5 4
ISBN 9780448486611 (hc)   10 9 8 7 6 5 4 3 2 1

The books in the Here's Hank series are designed using the font Dyslexie. A Dutch graphic designer and dyslexic, Christian Boer, developed the font specifically for dyslexic readers. It's designed to make letters more distinct from one another and to keep them tied down, so to speak, so that the readers are less likely to flip them in their minds. The letters in the font are also spaced wide apart to make reading them easier.

Dyslexie has characteristics that make it easier for people with dyslexia to distinguish (and not jumble, invert, or flip) individual letters, such as: heavier bottoms (b, d), larger than normal openings (c, e), and longer ascenders and descenders (f, h, p).

This fun-looking font will help all kids—not just those who are dyslexic—read faster, more easily, and with fewer errors. If you want to know more about the Dyslexie font, please visit the site www.dyslexiefont.com.

CHAPTER 1

"What rhymes with 'orange'?"
I asked my best friend Frankie
Townsend. We were sitting in
Riverside Park having an after-
school snack.

"Nothing," he said. "There isn't
one word in the English language
that rhymes with 'orange.'"

"How about '*borange*'?"
I asked.

My other best friend, Ashley
Wong, burst out laughing.

"Can I just point out that

'*borange*' isn't a word in any language?" she said.

"Then I give up." I threw my hands in the air. "Writing poetry is too hard. I quit."

Our teacher, Ms. Flowers, had told us the day before that everyone in our class had to write a poem about nature. We were going to read them at the We Love Nature assembly on Monday in the auditorium. Frankie and Ashley wrote theirs right away. They never have a problem at school in any subject. I have a problem with every subject. I'm bad at reading, spelling, math, and science. But I'm great at lunch.

The night before I had sat

at my desk forever, staring at a blank piece of paper. There wasn't a poem in my head or anywhere else in my body. So this morning my mom suggested that we all go to the park after school. She said that maybe looking at the flowers and trees would help me come up with an idea.

But it wasn't working.

"Hank, you can't just give up," my mom said. "You have an assignment to write a poem. Quitting is not a choice."

"Okay, Mom," I said. "I'll try one more time."

"Look around you and enjoy nature," she said. "Something will come to you."

I concentrated on some bright purple flowers. They were just starting to bloom.

"Okay, I've got the first lines for a poem," I said. "Ashley, would you please write these down when I say them?"

Ashley took a pencil from behind her ear and pulled out her little spiral notebook that was covered in rhinestones.

"I'm ready. Let it rip."

I cleared my throat and began:

*"Oh pretty flowers so bright
    and purple . . .
I love your smell, it is so
    gurple."*

When I got to the end, I noticed that Ashley had stopped writing.

"I've got to hand it to you, Zip," Frankie said. "'Purple' is the only other word I can think of that doesn't rhyme with anything."

"What about '*gurple*'?" I said. "That rhymes."

"But it's not a word," Ashley said.

I sighed loudly. This was just too frustrating.

"I think the problem, honey," my mom said, "is that you're not inspired. Do you know what 'inspired' means?"

"I do," Ashley said. "It means you're full of thoughts and ideas, and they just come pouring out."

"How am I supposed to get inspired about some purple flowers?" I asked.

"I think we need to take you out into *real* nature," my mom said. "I know a beautiful campsite a few hours north of the city called Harmony Acres. I'll bet you could write a poem there. Maybe we could go this weekend."

"Cool! Could we sleep over?" I asked. "In a tent and everything?

Can Frankie and Ashley come?"

"I can't," Ashley said. "It's my grandmother's birthday this weekend."

"But I'd love to come, if it's okay with my parents," Frankie said.

"We have to talk to Hank's dad," my mom said. "If he says yes, we'll leave Saturday morning."

"Let's go talk to Dad," I said. "This is going to be great."

We jumped up and hurried home. My dad was sitting at the dining-room table staring at his computer. He works at home. There's a desk in the bedroom where he's supposed to work, but he says he thinks better when he's dipping pretzels in sour cream. Mom doesn't like

pretzel crumbs all over the
bedroom rug, so he spends a lot
of time in the dining room.

"Dad! Dad!" I said as I raced
in. "We want to go on a family
camping trip!"

"Have a wonderful time, Hank.
I can't wait to hear all the
details. I'll be right here."

"No, Dad! The whole family is
going. That means you, too!"

My dad looked over at my mom.
He didn't look happy.

"Whose idea was this?"
he asked her.

"Well, Hank needs to write
a nature poem by Monday," she
said. "And I thought that being
out in nature would inspire him."

"You don't have to drive all
the way upstate to write a poem,"
he said.

"But I need to smell the trees
to be inspired," I told him.

"Nonsense, Hank. I can write
a poem without getting up from
this table."

He took one of his mechanical
pencils out of his pocket protector.
He always has three pencils lined
up in a row, in case one of them
runs out of lead. He stared at it

for a second and made up a poem on the spot.

"*A pencil like this sure comes in handy.*

But don't you eat it like cotton candy.

Use it to write your ABC's.

Then write your poem . . .

who needs trees?"

"Wow, Dad!" I said. "That's terrific. You're a poet and you didn't even know it!"

"You see, Hank? Who needs camping?"

My sister, Emily, wandered in. As usual, she was carrying her pet iguana, Katherine, around her neck like a scarf.

"Did I hear the word 'camping'?"

she asked. "Katherine doesn't like to camp out. Sleeping bags make her scales itch."

"For the first time ever, I agree with Katherine," my dad said.

"But, Dad," I said, "you don't have scales. At least not that I can see."

"I was talking about camping," he said. "I'm a city guy. I need pavement under my feet."

My mom put her hand on his shoulder. "This is just for one night, Stan. We'll sleep under

the stars and sit around the fire
and tell stories."

"And swat bugs," my dad added.

I took a deep breath. "Dad,"
I began, "you're always telling me
that I don't do well in school."

"That's because you don't try
hard enough, Hank."

"And also because you put
pencils in your ears instead of
listening to the teacher," Emily
chimed in.

Katherine shot her tongue out
at me and started to hiss. She
always takes Emily's side.

"Emily," my mom said. "Please
let Hank finish. You too, Katherine."

"I want to try harder," I said
to my dad. "And here is a chance

for me to finally do well. Think about it. We're at the We Love Nature assembly on Monday.
I stand up to read my poem. It's great, and the crowd goes wild. My teacher gives me an A. And you were part of it, because you said yes to camping."

Everyone was quiet for a minute. I think they were impressed with my speech. To be honest, I was, too.

My dad took off his glasses and put them in his shirt pocket. He stared at me for what seemed like a month and a half.

"I'll think about it," he said, "but don't hold your breath."

That wasn't exactly a yes. But it wasn't exactly a no, either.

CHAPTER 2

FOUR REASONS I GAVE MY DAD FOR WHY WE SHOULD ALL GO CAMPING

BY HANK ZIPZER

1. All that fresh air would help my feet grow into a new shoe size. (He said, "Shoes are expensive. Who wants to buy new ones?")

2. All that fresh air would feed my brain, and then maybe I could finally learn to do subtraction.

9 - 5 =
7 - 3 =
8 - 6 =
6 - 1 =
5 - 2 =

(He said, "I have subtraction
worksheets that you haven't
even started yet.")

3. All that fresh air would make
   me so hungry, I'd want to eat
   all the broccoli we always
   have at dinner. (He said
   broccoli gives him gas.)

4. All that fresh air would give us
   a chance to go for a really nice
   father-son hike. (That one got
   him. He thought about it, sighed,
   and finally said, "All right, Hank,
   I'll go.")

CHAPTER 3

On Saturday morning, we brought all our bags down to the lobby where Papa Pete and Frankie were waiting for us.

"Thanks for letting us borrow your car, Papa Pete," I said.

"My pleasure," he answered, handing the keys to my dad. "I filled it up with gas, so you're ready to roll."

"Are you sure this car can make the trip?" he asked. "I don't want it to break down on the side of the highway."

"This old car loves the highway," Papa Pete said. "I've taken it on a lot of road trips."

"That's my point," my dad said. "Who knows if it has one more road trip in it? So why take a chance? Let's forget the trip and all go to a Saturday afternoon movie. What do you say, kids?"

"I say camping." Then I started to chant, "Camping, camping, camping." Frankie and Emily joined in. My mom laughed. It looked like my father was going to cry.

"Seems like you have your answer, Stan," my mom said. "Let's load up the car and go."

We all helped put our stuff in the trunk. When it was almost full, my dad suddenly stopped and slapped his forehead.

"Wait a minute," he said. "I can't go. What about Cheerio? I have to take care of him. He's just a puppy."

"Remember that Mrs. Fink in apartment 10C has agreed to walk and feed Cheerio twice a day?" my mom said.

"But what happens if she can't find her false teeth? She won't leave her apartment. That happened once, and we didn't see her for three days. No, I can't risk that. I'm staying home with Cheerio. Have a great time, everyone."

He ran into the lobby. I followed him and found him pushing the elevator button over and over again.

"Dad, you just gave me a great idea," I said. "We'll take Cheerio. It will be the biggest adventure of his little puppy life."

"You can't take a dog into the wilderness," my dad said as the elevator doors opened.

"Of course you can," I said as we got in the elevator. "They're animals. They love wilderness."

I didn't stop talking until we were inside our apartment.

"Cheerio!" I called. "Want to go on a road trip?"

Cheerio jumped off the couch and almost flew into my arms.

"See?" I said to my dad. "He wants to go. How can we say no to this face?"

Cheerio looked over at my dad, and I swear he smiled right at him. That cute doggy's smile can even melt my dad's heart.

"Fine," he said, sighing deeply. "I'll let Mrs. Fink know what we're doing. Hank, get Cheerio's things together."

Everyone cheered when we came out of our building with Cheerio.

Emily reached out and scratched Cheerio under the chin.

"You are not as cute as my Katherine, and you can't catch flies with your tongue. But I'm glad you're coming along, anyway."

My mom hugged Dad and smiled.

"You did the right thing, Stan," she said. "You'll see. We're going to have a great time."

My dad just grunted like a hippo stuck in the mud.

We piled into the car. As

I was getting in, Papa Pete handed
me a brown paper bag.

"Here's a little surprise for
you kids," he said.

I didn't even have to open
the bag to know what was inside.
It was pickles, Papa Pete's favorite
snack. We always have a pickle
together when we've got a big
problem to solve.

"I brought a pickle for each of
you kids," he said. "Just don't let
Cheerio get them."

"Thanks, Papa Pete," we all said. Frankie calls him Papa Pete, too, even though he's not his grandfather.

"See you tomorrow," my mom called to Papa Pete.

"Don't forget to put on bug spray," he replied as he waved good-bye.

We took off. Mom and Dad sat up front. The three of us were in the backseat. Well, make that the four of us because I had Cheerio on my lap. As we drove out of the city, Frankie, Emily, and I played this game where you count red cars. By the time we were an hour out of the city, I had counted forty-three. Or maybe it was sixty-one. My brain isn't very good at keeping track of numbers.

"I don't think Cheerio likes the car ride," Frankie said as we sped along the highway. "He keeps breathing in my face, and his breath smells like pickles."

"Pickles!" I whispered. "Oh no! Cheerio, you didn't!"

"You better check the bag fast," Frankie said.

I reached down and felt around on the seat for the paper bag. The top was chewed open. That wasn't a good sign. When I looked inside, the signs were even less good. There was just

an empty plastic wrapper and
some pickle juice floating around
in it.

"Um . . . Dad . . . ," I said.
"I think we have to pull over."

"I'd rather not," my dad
answered. "We're almost there."

"I think it's pretty important,
Mr. Z.," Frankie said. "Cheerio
needs to use the restroom . . .
in a very pickle kind of way."

"What's that supposed to
mean?" my dad asked.

"He's going to barf, Dad,"
Emily said.

My dad pulled the car over to
the side of the road faster than
you can say *pickle chunks*.

My dad just stood by the side

of the road holding his head in
his hands.

"This is going to be okay,
Dad," I said, trying to cheer
him up.

"Hank, any trip that starts
with a dog throwing up is not
going to go well."

And you know what? He wasn't
all wrong.

CHAPTER 4

When Cheerio was feeling
better, we piled back into the car.
My father warned us that we were
not stopping anymore until we
got to the campsite. My mom was
holding a map and looking for the
right exit.

"Oh, there it is," she said,
pointing to a faded wooden sign
on the side of the highway. "It
says 'Harmony Acres, next right.'"

"Good work, Mom," I said.

"I'd be more comfortable if it

were a big sign with blinking lights that said 'this way to the city,'" my dad said.

"Now, Stan." My mom was using her extra-calm voice, the one she uses when I've forgotten my lunch for the third day in a row. "We're in nature. They don't want to clutter up the view with flashy signs."

"What view?" my dad said. "All I see is trees and sky."

"That's the point, Dad," Emily said. "We're out here exploring nature."

"Yeah," I said. "It's just us and the bears."

"Bears? What bears?" my dad asked. We were heading down

the highway ramp past the Harmony Acres sign. The car came to a sudden stop.

"Don't worry, Mr. Z.," Frankie piped up. "I read that if we keep our food tied up in a tree, the bears won't come into camp."

"Oh, look," my dad said, pointing to a few buildings out the window.

"How sweet," my mom said. "It's a cute little general store."

"I'm not looking at the store," my dad said. "I'm looking at what's connected to it. The Half Moon Motel. We could pull right in. Set up our tent in the middle of the room. I bet it's got cable TV and no bears."

"But, Dad," I said, "I'm not
supposed to write a poem about the
inside of a motel room. My poem is
about what it's like to be outside."

"Come on, Stan," my mom
said. "Nothing bad is going to
happen to us. We're going to
make a family memory."

For the twentieth time that
morning, my dad sighed. I couldn't
believe he had that much air in him.

He turned right onto a dirt
road. It seemed like we were on
that road forever. We passed

some farms with real live cows
munching on grass.

"Okay, everybody," my dad
called out. "Roll up the windows,
unless you enjoy the smell of
cow poop, which I don't."

For the first time that morning,
I totally agreed with him. The
cow-poop smell was hanging
around the inside of my nose
like stinky cheese.

After we passed the farms,
we headed up a hill with trees on
both sides of the road. Some of
the trees had white bark, and
others looked like Christmas trees.

"Maybe I'll write a poem
about a tree," I said. I opened
my mouth and this flew out:

"I see you, you big round tree.
I see you're much, much taller
than me.

"Hey, I did it!" I shouted. "It rhymes and everything. Did I just do my homework?"

"You sure did, Hank," my dad said. "This was certainly a great idea coming out here to nature. Now let's go home."

"If Hank wrote that here in the car," Emily said, "imagine what he can come up with when we're actually sleeping under the stars."

"I can't wait to see what our

campsite looks like," Frankie said. "I hope there's a fire pit so we can make s'mores."

"I've read all the brochures," my mom said. "It sounds like it has everything we're going to need."

"Except a heater, a bed, a refrigerator, and a TV," my dad muttered.

We drove the rest of the way without talking, just looking out the window. The road got smaller, the trees got taller, and the clouds got darker.

"You don't think it's going to rain, do you?" my dad said. "Because I don't do well in mud."

"I checked the weather forecast before we left," my mom said.

"There was no mention of rain."

We passed a red-and-white sign that I couldn't read, but Frankie could.

"Fire danger," he said, pointing to it.

My mom put her finger to her lips and made the *shhh* sound. Then she pointed to my dad.

"Oh," Frankie whispered to her.

We drove around a big bend in the road, and at last, there it was. Harmony Acres.

Let me just say, it was not exactly what we were expecting. There was a cabin at the entrance that only had three walls. The fourth one was lying in pieces on the ground next to it.

I looked through the trees to see if I could find any other cabins. Nope, there weren't any. There were just a bunch of wooden platforms scattered around. There was a gravel parking lot, but it didn't have any cars in it.

"Oh, isn't this wonderful?" my mom said in her extra-calm voice. "Looks like we'll have the place all to ourselves."

From out of nowhere, a man appeared and walked up to our

car. He was wearing a black-and-red checked shirt and baggy jeans with suspenders. His gray beard was so long,  it practically touched his knees.

"Howdy, folks," he said with a big smile. "I'm Jed Presley, no relation to Elvis. I'm the groundskeeper here. It's good to see you. We don't get many visitors this time of year. Bug season, you know."

"Oh, so that's why Papa Pete told us to take bug spray," I said.

"Where do we set up our tent?" my mom asked.

"Anywhere you don't see bear tracks," he answered.

My dad gasped so loud, I'm sure that everyone in China heard him.

"Just pulling your leg." Jed laughed, punching my dad on the arm. "We don't have bears here. We got a family of possums. You'll see them walking down to the lake after dark."

"Possums?" my dad asked. "I don't like the sound of that. They're like big rats."

"They're not rodents, Dad," Emily said. "They're marsupials. Did you know that they have thumbs on their back feet?"

"Thumbs on their feet?" I said. "Aren't those called toes?"

Frankie cracked up, but Emily, the little know-it-all, didn't even smile.

"Hank," she groaned. "You don't know anything about animal science."

"Well, I know about trees," I said. "I happen to have written a poem about them. And I say, let's set up our tent on that platform over there, under that big old tree."

"You folks have a great time," Jed said. "Camping out is good family fun."

"We'll get in touch with you if we need anything," my dad said.

"You do that," Jed said. "I'll be back in the morning."

"Wait, you're not staying here?" my dad said.

"I'm picking up supplies in town,"

Jed answered. "Remember, safety first. Put out your fire before you go to sleep. And be sure to tie your food up in a tree so the critters can't get to it."

"Could you *please* not say critters?" my dad said. But Jed was already walking away.

We unloaded the car. Everyone had the responsibility of carrying their own bag, except for Cheerio. All he had to carry was his little tennis ball with a bell in it.

Dad carried the tent. When we got all our gear onto the wooden platform, we heard a buzzing sound. We looked in every direction and saw nothing. Then we looked up.

Tucked in the top branches of the tree was a gray basket-like thing with a small opening at the bottom. It looked like it was made of thread. And it was buzzing.

"Wow!" Emily said. "A nest of yellow jackets! I've always wanted to see one."

We all looked up and saw lots of yellow jackets flying in and out of the nest. My dad's eyes grew as big as flying saucers.

"Yellow jackets?" he said.

"Aren't they like bees? Don't they sting?"

"Well, of course they do, Dad," Emily said. "It's how they defend themselves."

"I've read that they won't bother us if we don't bother them," my mom said. I could tell my mom was trying to keep him calm.

"Well, they're not going to bother me," my dad said, "because I am out of here!"

And without waiting for any of us, he took off running as fast as he could.

CHAPTER 5

Halfway to the parking lot, my dad stopped dead in his tracks.

"The bags," he shouted.
"I forgot the bags."

He turned around and ran back to where we were still standing. He grabbed all the bags we had brought and threw them over his shoulders. He looked like a stack of duffel bags with a head. Bags were hanging off every part of him. It was amazing that he could walk with all that stuff on him, let alone run. He took off again, heading for the parking lot.

"Dad, where are you going?" I yelled.

"As far away from those stingers as I can get!" he shouted back.

We followed him and didn't stop until we reached the car.

"Okay," he said, panting. "This has been a fun trip. Who's ready to head back? I know I am."

"There's no reason to leave," my mom said.

"How about a nest of buzzing, stinging insects?" he said. "That seems like a pretty good reason to me."

"Calm down, Stan," my mom

said. "We'll just set up our camp under another tree."

"Look, there's a great spot down by the lake," I said.

Without waiting for my dad's answer, we all headed for the clearing by the lake. Cheerio whined a little as we walked. I thought maybe his tummy was still pickle sick, so I picked him up and carried him under my arm.

"Hey, isn't this where that groundskeeper said the possums come at night?" Frankie asked me.

I gave him our special signal to be quiet, the one where you just slightly wave your hand under your chin. I didn't want my dad to hear what we were saying. I knew that possum talk would push him right back to the city.

We picked out a wooden platform at the lake's edge far from the yellow jackets' nest.

It was a lot of work to set up our campsite. Emily took Dad's hand and led him into the woods to gather sticks to make a fire in the fire pit. Mom took the food out of the cooler. Cheerio helped her.

Actually, he didn't exactly help her, but he did eat two raw hot dogs directly out of the package.

"Any poems popping into your head?" Frankie asked me as we sat down on the edge of our platform.

"Funny you ask," I said to him. "I was just trying to think of words that rhyme with 'yellow jacket.'"

"Did you come up with anything?"

"Yup, I sure did. *Jello shacket.* Or *pellow packet*. And then there's *wellow wacket*."

"Tell you what, Zip," Frankie
said. "Maybe we should try
putting up the tent. Give that
brain of yours a rest."

"Good idea," I said. "It's been
working very hard these last few
minutes."

I had never put up a tent
before, and following the
instructions was not easy.
There were lots of pictures

of hands pushing rods through
loops. No matter which way
I held the instruction sheet,
it looked upside down to me.

"How about I read the
instructions and tell you what
to do," Frankie suggested. "You
just listen and do it."

I nodded.

"Okay, first find the tarp and
lay it on the ground flat. That's
our ground sheet."

I laid the blue plastic tarp out
on the wood platform. That was
pretty easy.

"Now you take those rods
and put them together to make
two long poles," Frankie read.

I did that, too. It wasn't

that hard, either. I was getting the feel for this camping thing.

"Okay, Frankie," I said. "Got it. What's next?"

"Put the rods through the flaps in the tent so they cross each other at the top."

I could hardly believe it myself, but I could do that, too.

"Now what?"

"The instruction sheet just says that now you raise the tent and it will pop up."

"I have no idea how to do that," I said. "Maybe you say a magic word or something."

"Try *zengawii*," Frankie said, using his magic word.

I stood over the tent, waved my arms in a circle, and yelled, "*Zengawii!*"

I chanted it seven or eight times. Nothing happened. Well, something happened. My mom came over and found a little cord that was attached to the top of the tent. She pulled it up, and the tent came with it.

"It worked!" Frankie and I both said.

By that time, Emily and my dad had returned from the woods. Emily was up to her chin in sticks and twigs, and my dad had three or four big logs.

"There better not be spiders living in these," he said.

"Great job!" my mom said, ignoring his comment. "All that wood will make a wonderful fire."

"This wasn't easy," Emily whispered to Frankie and me.

"Dad was talking to snakes the whole time we were in the woods."

"Whoa, did you see a snake?" I asked.

"No, not one," Emily answered. "But Dad kept talking to them, anyway. He had twenty-five ways of saying 'leave me alone,' including 'back off,' 'keep your distance,' and 'if I see one forked tongue, I'm calling the Intergalactic Snake Patrol.'"

We laughed until our sides hurt, which is unusual when you're around Emily. She doesn't exactly tickle your funny bone.

My dad put the wood in the fire pit and looked around our

platform. When he saw the tent, his eyes nearly popped out of his head.

"We're not all sleeping in that, are we?" he asked. "There's no room."

"Come on, honey," my mom said. "We'll all put down sleeping bags and it'll be very cozy."

"And what if Cheerio burps all night?" he asked. "He's going to fill the tent with stinky pickle air."

We all cracked up again, but my dad didn't. He wasn't joking. In fact, he was in the worst mood that I'd ever seen him in— even worse than when I brought home my last report card with

the F in spelling and the D-minus
in math.

As the day went on, his mood
got worse, if you can believe
that. When we grilled hot dogs
for dinner, he ate standing up
because he was sure there were
spiders waiting to bite his rear end.
When he walked to the outdoor
bathrooms to brush his teeth, he
came running back screaming.

"Remember those possums?"
he yelled. "I know where they

live. In the men's bathroom."

And when we all piled into the tent and got in our sleeping bags, my dad shot out of his like a rocket.

"What was that creepy thing I felt on my shoulder?" he screamed.

"Stan, that was just my hand," my mom said. "I was saying good night. Do you think you're going to be able to sleep at all?"

"I'm not even going to try," he said. "I'm going to keep my eyes wide open all night."

My mom sat up and turned on the battery-operated lantern she had bought for our trip.

"Mom, turn off the light," Emily whined. "I can't sleep. And look, you woke up Cheerio."

"I think none of us is going
to get any sleep with your father
being so upset," my mom said.
"So I have a suggestion."

"I hope it has to do with going
home," my dad said.

"We can't go back, Dad,"
I said. "I haven't written my poem
yet."

"So here is my idea," my mom
said. "Stan, we're fine here. And
I think you should get in the car
and drive down to the Half Moon
Motel that we passed on the way

up. You can sleep in a spider-free bed and take a possum-free shower, and we'll see you tomorrow morning for breakfast."

"Are you sure you'd be okay?" my dad said.

"We're fine," she said. "Look at us. All tucked in safe and sound. Aren't we, kids?"

"Yes," we all said together. We knew that the only way we'd get any sleep at all was to let my father go.

He kissed us each good-bye and practically ran up the hill to the car. We heard the engine start and the wheels crunch on the gravel driveway. As we listened to the sound of his car driving away, we settled into our sleeping bags for the night.

The sounds inside our tent were so cool. We could hear the water lapping against the shore of the lake, an owl hooting in the distance, Cheerio snoring. I felt positive that a great poem was going to come into my mind.

It was all so peaceful, the perfect outdoor adventure.

I closed my eyes and snuggled deep into my sleeping bag. I was almost asleep when I heard a noise. *What was that?*

Something was rustling just outside our tent.

CHAPTER 6

I poked my head out of my sleeping bag and whispered to Frankie.

"Are you awake? Did you hear that?"

"Yes, I did."

"Do you think it's an animal?"

"It's just a little wind in the trees," Frankie said.

"Well, it doesn't sound like a little wind to me," I whispered back.

"Go to sleep, Zip," Frankie

said. "Your ears don't work when you're asleep."

Frankie rolled over and pulled his sleeping bag up around his neck. I rolled over the other way and pulled my sleeping bag over my ears. But that didn't block out the sound, which was growing louder by the minute. I could hear the wind blowing so hard, the branches on the trees were starting to creak. In the darkness, I heard Emily's voice.

"Hank, it's really windy out there," she said. "Do you think one of those trees could fall down on us?"

"Relax, Emily," I said. "It's just a little wind."

I tried to sound like a calm older brother, but even to me, my voice sounded like a scared little kid.

"I'll check to make sure our tent is tied down tight," my mom said, crawling out of her sleeping bag. "There could be a little storm coming. Nothing to worry about."

As she unzipped the tent flap and stepped outside, a giant blast of wind came whistling into our tent. It blew so hard, it almost lifted Cheerio's ears off his head. But good old Cheerio slept right through it. I think his bad pickle experience had worn him out.

Through our flapping tent door, I could see my mom outside testing the cords that held our tent to the wooden platform.

When she came back in, her hair looked like she hadn't combed it for a month. It looked like a lion's mane, but not in a good way.

"Whoa," she said, trying to smooth down her hair with her hands. "It's really blowing hard out there. And I felt a few raindrops."

"Is our tent waterproof?"
Emily asked.

"Sure it is," my mom said.
"Besides, even if we get wet,
a little rain never hurt anyone.
We're not going to melt."

Without anyone saying anything,
we all pulled our sleeping bags
into a tighter circle. We listened
to the raindrops *pitter-patter*
on the top of our tent.

It wasn't so bad, until the
pitter-patter turned into *ka-boom*,
ka-boom. I don't know how big
those raindrops were— but they
sounded like they were the size
of soccer balls. And the wind
was going crazy. It was like
a train going through a tunnel.

"Hey, kids," my mom said, sounding extremely fake cheerful. "This is even more of an adventure than we thought we'd have. Hank, I'll bet this rain is giving you all sorts of ideas for your poem."

"Yeah," Frankie said. "What rhymes with 'storm'?"

"'Warm,'" I said with a shiver. "Which I'm definitely not."

"I'm scared," Emily said. "Mommy, can I get in your sleeping bag?"

"Of course you can," she said, sliding over to make room for Emily.

"Can Cheerio come, too?" Emily asked.

"I'll put him in my sleeping bag," I said.

I picked up Cheerio and tucked him in right next to me. That was a mistake, because as soon as he got in my sleeping bag, he farted. I don't want to say it smelled bad, but let's just say it was like lying inside a jar of old pickles.

I unzipped my sleeping bag a little to let in some fresh air. All of a sudden, a big gust of wind hit our tent so hard that the sides actually started to flutter. The sound of the tent flapping got really loud. It sounded like the tent was going to take off like a small plane.

"Mrs. Z.!" Frankie shouted over the howling wind. "This doesn't seem like a little storm to me. I'm kind of scared."

I've known Frankie Townsend since preschool, and I've never heard him say he was scared. That was enough to scare me— even more than I already was.

"Don't worry, kids. I'm sure this storm will blow over quickly. And besides, our tent is very secure."

As soon as my mom said those words, a burst of wind attacked our tent and almost lifted it right off the wooden platform. Correct that. It DID

lift it right off the wooden
platform, like a helium balloon.
Cheerio woke up and started to
bark at the sky. I would have
joined him if I thought it would
do any good. Instead, the four
of us sat there getting totally
soaked and watched our tent
tumble away toward the lake.

"What do we do now?"
I heard Emily scream.

That was the best question
I had ever heard her ask.

CHAPTER 7

The rain was pounding down on us. And to make things worse, fog was rolling in, as thick as pea soup with ham. I tried to follow the path of our tent as it rolled down the hill toward the lake. It was hard to see with all the fog and the rain.

We were soaking wet, and even our sleeping bags were getting soggy.

"I'll go down the hill and get our tent," Mom said. "Everyone stay just where you are."

"No!" Emily screamed. "Don't leave me, Mommy."

Emily threw her arms around my mom. She held on so tight, she almost put her in a headlock. That girl could be a wrestler on TV. It was clear my mom wasn't going anywhere without Emily attached to her like a fanny pack.

"I'll go after the tent," I said. I couldn't believe that those words had come out of my mouth. But there they were.

"Frankie!" I yelled over the wind. "You stay here and stand guard. Cheerio, you come with me."

Cheerio yipped and looked at me as if to say, "You've got to be kidding. Do I look like I'm wearing a raincoat?"

He dived into my sleeping bag, and all I could see was the shape of a long body burrowing into the deep end of my bag.

"Okay, I guess it's just me," I said.

"Here, take the flashlight," my mom said, rummaging around in her duffel bag to find it. "And come right back with the tent."

"Don't worry," I said in the most confident voice I could come up with. "I'll handle this."

I turned on the flashlight and jumped off the wooden platform. What had been solid ground in the afternoon was now a sea of slippery mud. I'd like to say I landed on my feet, but I didn't. I'd like to say I landed on my knees, but I didn't. That leaves only one possibility, and you guessed it. I landed smack on my backside.

"You okay, Zip?" I heard Frankie call out.

"No problem," I hollered back. "I meant to do that."

Since I was already on the ground, I thought I'd just stay there and crawl the rest of the way. I waded through the mud on my hands and knees. Every few feet, I'd stop and shine the flashlight ahead of me, looking in the distance for our tent. The flashlight didn't help much, because all it did was light up the fog.

Just keep going forward, I said to myself. *You can't be scared now. Everyone is counting on you.*

It's too bad that I was too nervous to answer myself.

I continued crawling down the muddy hill, trying to listen for the sound of a flapping tent. I was so busy listening that I crawled right into a big puddle of muddy water. I lost my balance and dropped the flashlight. I reached out to search for it, digging my hands into the mud in front of me. I grabbed on to something that I hoped was the flashlight, but it wasn't! It was long and thin and slimy.

"Yikes! A snake!" I yelled as I pulled it out of the ground.

It took me a few seconds to realize the snake wasn't moving. That's because it wasn't a snake at all. But it was a snake-shaped old tree root, so you can't blame me for being a little scared.

I decided to leave the flashlight behind. Through the howling wind, I thought I heard the tent flapping in the distance. I had to get to it. Just the thought of my mom and Emily and Frankie sitting out in the open was enough to push me forward.

I crawled past swaying trees and empty campsites. Up ahead, I saw the shadowy outline of something wide and dark. Because of the thick fog, I couldn't make out what it was. It could have been our tent. Or it could have been a bear. I stopped moving and held my breath, waiting for it to roar.

It flapped instead.

Phew! It was our tent!

I crawled toward it at top speed. I don't think I've ever crawled so fast in my life, not even when I was a baby. Just before I reached the tent, another gust of wind blew so hard, it snapped off a tree branch. I rolled over in the mud just in time for the branch to land on the ground next to me.

I scrambled to my feet and lunged at the tent, grabbing at it so hard I fell over on it. I heard another snap, but this time it wasn't a tree branch. It was the plastic poles that held our tent up, breaking in two. It didn't matter, though. At least I had the tent in my hands.

I turned and started up the hill, my legs ankle-deep in mud. The mud was so thick that I

could barely lift my feet out
to take the next step. I was
totally surprised when I realized
that my foot was out but my
shoe was still stuck under all
that muck.

Oh well, I thought, *one shoe
down, but I've still got the other
one. Onward, Hank!*

I headed up the path, struggling
to hold on to the tent as it
flipped and flopped in the wind.
It was slow going, but I was
making it. That is, until I saw
the two eyeballs glowing in the
dark on the path in front of me.
Suddenly, there were four eyeballs,
then six. Maybe there were more,
but I stopped counting at six.

Any creature with over six eyeballs
was definitely not one that
I wanted to meet.

"Excuse me, whoever you
are," I said, "but could you
please step off the path?
My family needs me."

Not one of the six eyeballs
moved. Obviously, the polite
approach wasn't working, so
I decided to make the loudest
noise my throat could make.

"Aarrgghhhuuugggaaahhhh!"
I shouted.

I squinted hard, trying to see
the creature through the fog.
At last it came into focus. It was
a family of possums, just standing
in the middle of the path.

"*Zengawii!*" I yelled. "Possums, disappear!"

They didn't disappear, but what they did do was good enough for me. At the sound of my screaming voice, they rolled over on their sides and played dead. They just lay there, not moving a muscle.

"Have it your way, guys," I said.

Grabbing the tent tightly, I ran past them. I glanced back, and they still weren't moving.

I scrambled up the last part

of the hill, slipping and sliding
in the mud. I squinted again,
trying to find the platform, but
I couldn't see that far in front
of me.

The fog was so thick, it was
like being in a dark gray cloud.
Then I saw it off to the left. Or
maybe it was the right. I'm not
good at directions. But, anyway,
I recognized our red-and-white
cooler sitting on the edge of
the wooden platform. As I got
closer, I could see something was
strange, though. Nobody was on
the platform.

"Mom!" I shouted. "Where
are you guys?"

But there was no answer.

CHAPTER 8

My heart started to race. Where were they? Had they left me alone out here? No, my mom would never do that. Oh no! Then maybe something had happened to them. Maybe they went looking for me and got lost in the soggy, foggy forest.

"Mom!" I shouted again. My voice echoed in the darkness. I could hear that I was starting to panic.

Then one of the sleeping

bags started to talk. I couldn't understand what it was saying, but it sounded like this.

"Schmank, schmank."

I'd never heard that word before. I wondered what it meant. Was it an alien language?

"Schmank," I whispered to myself. And then it hit me. *Schmank* rhymes with *Hank*. The sleeping bag was calling my name!

"I'm over here," I yelled. "Next to the platform."

Suddenly four heads popped out of the sleeping bags—Frankie, Emily, Cheerio, and my mom.

"Whoa, am I glad to see you guys!" I said, almost crying with relief. "Why were you hiding? Did you see a bear?"

"We were just trying to stay dry," my mom answered.

"I even made us hats out of wax paper," Emily said. "Cheerio hates wearing his."

"Did you find the tent, Hank?" Frankie asked. "No offense to you, Emily, but I think that will keep us drier than your wax-paper hats."

"Yes, I got it," I said, holding up the soaking tent.

"You are the best, Zip!" Frankie crawled out of his sleeping bag. "I never doubted you. Let's put it up right away."

"One small tent problem,"
I said. "I fell on it and broke it."

Suddenly, there was a gust of
wind followed by a giant burst
of hard rain. It was as if a cloud
above us had opened up and
emptied itself out. And then there
was a big crash. Our lantern was
broken now, too.

Emily screamed and dived back
into my mom's sleeping bag.

"Hank, how badly is the tent
broken?" my mom asked. "We
need shelter . . . now."

"I'll figure this out, Mom,"
I said. "You just take care of
Emily and Cheerio."

My mom disappeared back into
her sleeping bag, leaving Frankie

and me to build a shelter. I slipped
the tent poles out, hoping that at
least one of them hadn't broken.
No such luck. I had four short poles
that would be perfect if I were
building a tent for Cheerio. But
they sure wouldn't work to build
a tent that we could all fit into.

"If we could put all these
pieces together to make one long
pole, we could build some sort
of tepee," I suggested.

"Great thinking," Frankie said.
"That's using the old Zipzer brain.
Except how are we going to connect
the poles? You don't happen to
have any glue on you, do you?"

I looked around the platform,
searching for an idea. I saw Emily's

bag, our red-and-white cooler, Frankie's backpack, my dad's emergency kit, and my mom's knitting bag.

Wait a minute, Hank. Back up. Dad's emergency kit—maybe there's something in there that I could use.

I jumped across the platform, grabbed the kit, and unzipped it. There were enough first-aid supplies in there to open a hospital. Rubber gloves, batteries, needles and thread, light sticks, gauze, adhesive tape, anti-itch cream, a silver emergency blanket, and a pack of twenty-five Band-Aids of every size and shape. My dad always says "be prepared," and boy, was he ever!

I took the light
sticks, the Band-Aids,
the gauze pads, and
the adhesive tape and
ran back to Frankie.

"What's all that for?"
he asked.

"Dr. Zipzer reporting to
surgery," I said. "I'm going
to operate on the pole."

I snapped the center of one of
the light sticks. It put out a soft
green glow. That was good enough
for us to see what we were doing.
Frankie matched the four pieces
of pole together, while I ripped
open the gauze pads. I wrapped
a bunch of them around the spots
where the poles connected.

"You hold this tight," I told
Frankie. "Don't let go."

Then I grabbed the twenty-five
Band-Aids and tore each one out
of its wrapper. One by one, I peeled
the paper off the sticky parts and
placed them over the gauze until
I couldn't see it anymore.

"You can let go now," I told
Frankie. "It should hold."

"I don't think so, Zip. The
connection is still too weak.
I think we need to double it up
with adhesive tape."

"Okay," I said. "And maybe I can use the light stick as a splint."

I pulled out the roll of adhesive tape. Frankie held the light stick tightly against the pole, and I wrapped a whole lot of tape around it, making sure I left enough of the light unwrapped so we could still see. Between the gauze and the Band-Aids and the light stick and the adhesive tape, we had made one long pole.

"Here we go," I said. "One tepee coming up."

We propped the pole up using all our duffel bags. Then we threw the tent over the pole. We held one side down using the cooler and the other side with

Dad's emergency kit. For extra protection, we threw the thin silver emergency blanket over the top.

"That's one weird-looking tepee," Frankie said.

"True," I agreed. "Let's hope that it works."

I stuck my head inside. It was dry. No rain was getting through.

"Mom!" I yelled. "We've got shelter. Come on out!"

My mom crawled out of her sleeping bag holding Emily's hand. I noticed that Emily's braids were dripping like a leaky water faucet.

"Our tepee doesn't look like much," I explained, "but it works."

"You did a great job, boys," she said.

My mom led Emily across the platform. I held part of the tepee up high enough for them to crawl in.

"Cheerio!" I called. "Come on, puppy!"

I saw a small moving lump scooting along inside the sleeping bag, then Cheerio's head popped out. He scampered out and started to run in circles.

"We don't have time for that now, Cheerio," I told him. "Get in here. No tail-chasing inside tepees."

Cheerio went into the tepee. Frankie and I followed him, closing the flap behind us. As soon as I sat down, Cheerio jumped in my lap and licked my face, as if to say *thank you, Hank.*

"What a relief," my mom said. "It's dry in here."

"But it's really dark, too," Emily said in a little voice.

"Perfect for telling ghost stories," Frankie told her. "Anyone got one?"

"I do," I said. I cleared my throat and lowered my voice to a whisper. "It was a dark and stormy night in Ghostville—just like this one."

Before I could get another sentence out, our whole tepee was lit up by two beams of light.

"Uh-oh," I said. "We are not alone."

"Mommy," Emily said, her voice sounding very little and shaky.

"Who's there?" I called out.

But the only answer I got was the sound of the wind howling through the trees.

CHAPTER 9

A few seconds later, we heard a door slam, then footsteps sloshing through the mud. They were coming toward our tepee. I gulped. Cheerio buried his head in my lap, and Emily buried her head in my mom's lap.

"It's probably just the groundskeeper, Elvis What's-his-name," Frankie said.

"It's Jed What's-his-name," I answered.

The footsteps grew closer and closer.

"Where is everyone?" a voice called out.

Wait a minute. I knew that voice.

"We're in here, Dad!" I shouted.

"In where? I don't see the tent."

"It's a tepee now. Come in!"

I lifted a side and stuck my head out. My dad got down on his knees and crawled in.

"I was so worried," he said. "I should never have left you guys."

"Hank took very good care of us," my mom told him.

"The tent blew totally away," Emily chimed in, "and Hank went out in the dark and found it."

"I lost our flashlight, though, Dad. I'm sorry."

My dad reached out and put his arm around my shoulder.

"Don't you even think about that," he said. "You did a great job looking after everyone. I was the one who got scared, but you— you were the brave one. You showed a lot of courage. And you took responsibility. I'm so proud of you, son."

My ears nearly flew off my head. Usually my dad tells me that I need to take more responsibility. But here he was

telling me how proud he was of me. Wow, that made me so happy.

"Thanks, Dad," I said. "But I have to tell you that Frankie helped me a lot."

"I bet he did." My dad reached out and put his other arm around Frankie. "You boys are good friends."

"And the important thing is that we're all safe and dry and together," my mom said.

Just then, some rainwater dribbled in through the crack where the pole was attached to the tent.

"Well, pretty dry," I said.

"A little water never hurt anyone," my dad said. "We're not going to melt, are we, kids?"

"We could go back to the car for shelter," my mom said.

"We like it in here," Frankie and I said.

"Okay," my dad said. "Let's settle in until the rain stops. I'm not leaving you guys ever again."

We snuggled together in our tepee and listened to the rain. In the green glow of the light stick, it seemed very peaceful in there. Even my dad was calm.

"I have a great idea," my mom said after a while. "How about a little snack to take our minds off the rain." She looked around the tepee. "I don't see the red-and-white food cooler."

"We used it to hold down the tepee," Frankie said.

"Do you want me to go out and get stuff from it?" I asked.

"Thanks, Hank, but it's my turn," Dad said.

He crawled under the tepee flap, and I heard him rustling around in the cooler. When he returned, he was carrying plastic baggies filled with graham crackers, marshmallows, and chocolate squares.

"S'mores!" we cheered.

"Except we don't have a fire," Emily pointed out. "How

are we going to melt everything?"

"Don't tell me you've never heard of Zipzer's Famous Cold S'mores?" my dad said. "They're a treat known around the world."

"And we're going to make them now," my mom said. For the first time that night, she was actually laughing.

She gave each of us two graham crackers, two marshmallows, and two squares of chocolate.

"Now make a sandwich," she said.

We all did.

"And now comes the best part," she said. "Take a bite."

To be very honest, I like my s'mores better with a toasted

marshmallow and the
chocolate all melty
and smooth. But this

s'more was pretty special. As we
listened to the rain *drip-dropping*
on our tepee, I thought it was the
best midnight snack I'd ever had.
Suddenly, inspiration struck me. I
opened my mouth and this is what
came out:

"Oh little s'more
That I eat on the floor,
You make me so warm and happy.
You give me joy
Even more than a toy
Because you're delicious and
    snappy."

Everyone stopped chewing and
looked at me.

"Listen to you, Zip," Frankie said. "That's an actual poem."

"You see, Hank. I told you that you could do it." My mom smiled.

"It's just a little poem," I said. "And it's not even about nature."

"But it's funny," Emily said. "And it rhymes."

"It's very cool," Frankie said. "I bet no one has ever written a poem about s'mores."

"You're having quite a night for yourself, Hank," my dad said. "You have a lot to be proud of."

As I reached for my second s'more, all I could do was grin. What had begun as a soggy, foggy disaster was turning out to be one of the best nights of my life.

CHAPTER 10

On Monday at two o'clock, all
the first- and second-graders at
PS 87 were sitting in the auditorium
waiting for the We Love Nature
assembly to begin. Because we
were the big kids, we got to sit in
actual chairs. The first-graders had
to sit on the floor in front of us.

All the parents were sitting
in the rest of the seats. All the
parents, that is, except my dad. He
had told me that morning that he
wasn't going to be able to come to

the assembly because of an important
business meeting. It was a long
story about his computer crashing,
most of which I didn't understand
because it involved words like "hard
drive," "double right-click," and
"lost documents." The part I did
understand, and I wished I didn't, was
that he wasn't going to be there.

Principal Love got the assembly
started by walking up to the
microphone and clearing his throat.
He rubbed the mole on his cheek,
which looks like the Statue of Liberty
without the torch. Then he began.

"Welcome, boys and girls, and parents of **PS** 87," he said. It sounded like he had a little frog in his throat. He could have used one more throat clearing before he spoke.

"Today we are celebrating nature," he said. "As we all know, nature is a natural part of our natural world, which is the world we naturally live in."

"He's not making any sense," Frankie whispered in my ear.

"He never does," Ashley whispered in the other ear.

"But it's a lot of fun to watch the mole bounce up and down on his cheek," I said. "It looks like it's doing the hula."

We all burst out laughing but

stopped immediately when Principal Love shot us that look that says "no laughing allowed."

Then he introduced our teacher, Ms. Flowers, who told the parents about our unit on writing nature poems. The parents all applauded when they heard we were going to read our poems out loud to them.

"Boys and girls," she said, "make sure you have your poem in your hand, ready to read."

"Uh-oh," I said, realizing that

I was the only one not holding my poem in my hand.

"Zip, tell me you didn't . . . ," Frankie said.

"Lose it," Ashley added.

"It's got to be here somewhere," I said, grabbing my backpack.

While the first students got up onstage to read their poems, I unzipped every compartment of my backpack in a wild search for my poem. Some of them twice. I found old gummy bears, pencils with no points, and erasers shaped like bananas. But no poem. I must have forgotten to put it in.

I really don't like my brain,
I thought. *It never remembers
what I need it to remember.*

"Hank Zipzer," I heard
Ms. Flowers saying. "Would you
please come to the stage and let
us all hear your poem?"

"I don't have it," I whispered
to Frankie.

"Then you have to do it from
memory," he said.

"Can you do that?" Ashley asked.

"I guess I'm going to find out
real quick."

I stood up slowly, trying to go over the lines in my head. As I crawled over the other kids to get to the aisle, Nick McKelty stuck his foot out to trip me. He is the biggest, thickest, meanest kid in all of second grade. His idea of a big laugh is tripping people and watching them fall down.

"Don't even bother going up there, Zipper Teeth," he said. "Your poem is going to stink up the place."

Usually I would have had a snappy comeback for him. But I wasn't feeling all that confident. I wasn't sure I had any poem—stinky or not.

I got to the stage and stood in front of the microphone. Wow, there were a lot of people out there in the auditorium. All the moms and dads were waving and trying to get their kid's attention. As I looked out over all the faces, I noticed the back door open. A man in a raincoat walked in. Inside that raincoat was my dad!

Whoa, he had made it after all!

When he saw me onstage, he got a giant grin on his face, and gave me a big thumbs-up.

That's all I needed. Before you could say "Zipzer's Famous Cold S'mores," the poem came flying out of my mouth, just like it had when I first made it up in our tepee. I was inspired! I felt like I had been born to write poems about s'mores.

When I was finished, all the kids applauded. Some of the parents looked a little surprised.

"Well, young man," Principal Love said. "That's a tasty poem, but I hardly think it's about nature."

"Actually, it is," I told him. "Because it was written in nature, in between a rainstorm and a possum family."

The entire audience burst out laughing. I looked over at my dad, and he was laughing, too. It felt pretty good.

"Hank," Ms. Flowers said. "You wrote a fine poem. It lets us all know just how wonderful it is to be out in nature around a campfire."

"Minus the fire," I said. "But it was still pretty wonderful."

"Poems are supposed to be original," she said. "And yours certainly is. Congratulations, Hank."

Out of the corner of my eye, I saw my father clap his hands. I think I even heard him yell, "Go, Hank!"

Everything got a little blurry after that. I'm not sure if anyone else was clapping or cheering. But my dad sure was, and that's all I needed.

CHAPTER 11

THE FOUR THINGS ABOUT POETRY I LEARNED FROM WRITING POETRY

BY HANK ZIPZER

1. Don't even try to rhyme anything with "orange" or "purple." It's not possible, unless you make up a crazy word like ka-burple.

2. Don't say NO to trying to write a poem. It can be pretty fun, especially if it involves marshmallows.

3. Double-check the weather report before you go on a camping trip.

4. Reading poems is fun. Here are three funny ones I discovered after my camping trip. Check them out: "Celery" by Ogden Nash, "Little Pig's Treat" by Shel Silverstein, and "I Made a Noise This Morning" by Jack Prelutsky.